This edition published 2010 by Zero to Ten Ltd,
Part of the Evans Publishing Group,
2A Portman Mansions,
Chiltern Street,
London, W1U 6NR

British Library Cataloguing in Publication Data
A CIP catalogue record for this book is available
from the British Library

ISBN: 9781840895834

Printed in China by New Era Printing Co. Ltd

Tall Tilly

by Jillian Powell

illustrated by Tim Archbold

ZERO TO TEN

Tilly was growing taller
every day.

She was taller than
all her friends.

She was the tallest girl
in her class.

She was too tall for
her clothes.

She was too tall for her bed.

She was too tall for the bath.

She was even too tall for Ben,
the boy she liked in class!

Worst of all, Tilly wanted
to be a ballerina.

But she was too tall.

Tilly hated it.

She wanted to be small
and dainty, like her
best friend, Molly.

Then Tilly's teacher had an idea.

She made Tilly Sports Captain.

Tilly was so tall that she scored lots of
goals for the basketball team…

...and she saved lots of goals for
the football team.

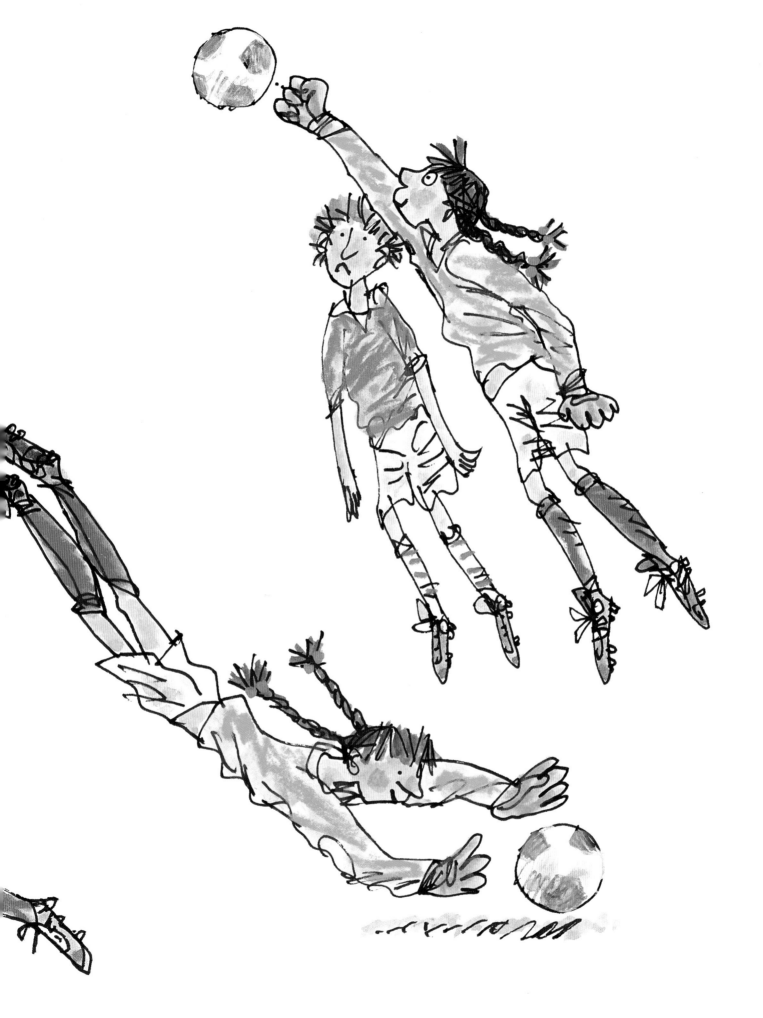

She was so tall she won
every running race.

She jumped the highest high jumps.

She jumped the longest long jumps.

Everyone cheered for her.

Tilly loved being tall after all!